This edition published by Parragon Books Ltd in 2014

Parragon Books Ltd
Chartist House
15–17 Trim Street
Bath BA1 1HA, UK
www.parragon.com

ISBN 978-1-4723-7980-1

Printed in China

Bath • New York • Cologne • Melbourne • Delhi
Hong Kong • Shenzhen • Singapore • Amsterdam

Marlin was a clownfish, but that didn't mean he had to find life funny.

Marlin had lost his wife and more than four hundred eggs in a ruthless barracuda attack. Only one egg had survived, but he had one damaged fin.

"I promise I will never let anything happen to you … Nemo," Marlin said.

After Nemo was born, Marlin wouldn't let him out of his sight. Marlin was so protective, he didn't even like him going beyond their sea anemone home. But, on Nemo's first day of school, Nemo was ready for adventure!

"Wake up, wake up! C'mon!" Nemo exclaimed, swimming circles around his sleeping father.

Before they set off for school, Marlin asked sternly, "What's the one thing we have to remember about the ocean?"

"It's not safe," Nemo sighed.

As they swam to school together, Marlin kept reminding Nemo to hold his fin.

Nemo had made some new friends from his class and they sneaked off together, daring each other to swim out into the open sea. Nemo was nervous and didn't venture very far, but it was way too far for Marlin, who was hovering nearby.

"You think you can do these things but you just can't!" Marlin shouted.

Nemo wanted to prove his dad wrong. He swam to a boat and hit it with his fin.

Suddenly, a diver appeared....

"Daddy! Help me!" Nemo screamed as he caught sight of his reflection in the diver's mask.

In a flash, the diver had scooped Nemo up in a net. Marlin raced to the surface as the divers sped away. There was nothing he could do to save his precious son. Their boat had sped off so quickly that a diver's mask had fallen overboard.

Marlin rushed to a busy underwater road to get help.

"Has anybody seen a boat?" he cried.

A beautiful blue tang named Dory told him that she had seen a boat! "Follow me!" she said.

However, Dory had a very bad memory. One minute later, she couldn't even remember why Marlin was following her!

"Will you quit it?" she asked.

Confused, Marlin turned to swim away. Only to come face to face with …

... a huge shark!

He was called Bruce and he was trying to be a vegetarian. He befriended Dory and Marlin and wanted them to meet his like-minded buddies, so they could prove their motto: "Fish are friends, not food!"

Dory, who was as enthusiastic as she was forgetful, thought it was a wonderful idea. Terrified Marlin did not.

The 'self-help' sharks held their meetings in a wrecked submarine.

"It has been three weeks since my last fish," Bruce told his friends proudly.

Always eager, Dory joined in. "I don't think I've ever eaten a fish."

Just then, Marlin spotted the diver's mask! Dory wanted to show it to the sharks but Marlin didn't.

As they tussled, Dory bumped her nose and it bled a little. Bruce got a sudden craving for a fish dinner!

As Dory and Marlin tried to escape something exploded!

Meanwhile, Nemo found himself in a dentist's fish tank in Sydney. He soon discovered how small the tank was when he crashed into the side.

A group of fish came out of hiding. Bubbles, Peach, Jacques, Bloat, Deb and Gurgle were thrilled to meet a fish from the open sea.

Later, Nemo learnt that he was to be a present for the dentist's niece, Darla.

"She's a fish-killer," whispered Peach.

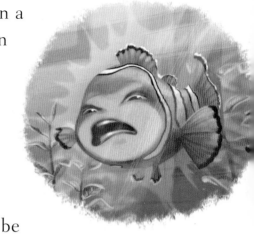

That night, a ceremony was held to make Nemo an official member of their group. All Nemo had to do was swim through the RING OF FIRE!

It sounded scary, but it was really just a stream of bubbles. Nemo bravely swam through the bubbles and into the gang's hearts.

Afterwards Gill, the leader of the tank announced, "From this moment on, you will now be known as 'Shark Bait'." Next, he revealed his plan to escape from the tank....

Back in the ocean, Dory had dropped the mask into a deep trench! She and Marlin swam after it and ran into an anglerfish.

Suddenly, Dory remembered she could read!

"P. Sherman, 42 Wallaby Way, Sydney," Dory read from the mask strap.

Thinking quickly, Marlin trapped the anglerfish inside the mask. The pair were so excited – they knew where to find Nemo!

Marlin told Dory he was going to Sydney alone.

"You mean you don't like me?" Dory asked.

A school of moonfish rushed over and were angry with Marlin for upsetting Dory. The moonfish told Dory how to get to Sydney. "Follow the East Australian Current," they said.

Then, they gave her a warning. "When you come to a trench, swim through it, not over it."

When they finally got to the trench, however, Marlin insisted that swimming over it would be much safer. Soon they were surrounded by stinging jellyfish! Dory thought it was fun to bounce on top of them! They had found a safe way through – but they were tired and had been stung by the jellyfish. They needed help.

Some sea turtles rescued Marlin and Dory. Their run-in with the jellyfish had left them in bad shape.

"Takin' on the jellies – awesome!" exclaimed Crush, a surfer turtle.

Marlin watched as Crush encouraged his children to be adventurous. He thought it taught them important lessons. Watching Crush's kids made Marlin wonder if he had been too protective of Nemo.

Tales of Marlin's adventures were spreading far and wide.

Nigel, a friendly pelican who knew the Tank Gang, eventually heard the stories and rushed to tell Nemo the incredible news.

Nemo was amazed. He had always thought his dad was a bit of a scaredy-fish. The thought that he was battling his way to Sydney filled the little fish with pride.

Nemo was inspired by his dad's bravery and he was determined to escape. To his friends' horror, Nemo darted into the filter and successfully jammed it! Everyone cheered!

Very soon, the tank gang was swimming in slimy, green water. They couldn't have been happier! Dr Sherman was going to have to clean the tank before Darla arrived!

Back in the ocean, Marlin and Dory said goodbye to the turtles, but soon found themselves swallowed up inside the mouth of a massive whale.

"It's okay, I speak Whale," Dory assured Marlin. "He either said we should move to the back of his throat, or he wants a root beer float," she translated.

It turned out the whale was only giving the two brave little fish a lift. They were soon squirted out of the whale's blowhole, right into Sydney Harbour!

They nearly ended up as breakfast for a hungry pelican, but
eventually they escaped ... and landed on the dock.

Luckily, Nigel rushed to their rescue.

"Hop inside my mouth if you want to live," he whispered.

Nigel snatched them up,
filled his beak with some
water and took off. The
hungry seagulls followed,
but Nigel played a trick on
them and the seagulls flew
right into a boat's sail!

Inside, the dentist had cleaned the tank water with a fancy new automated cleaner – while the fish were still in the tank!

The escape plan was ruined.

Nemo was lifted out of the tank and plopped into a bag. Darla had arrived. Nemo had one last chance – he played dead, hoping that he would get flushed down the toilet and out into the ocean.

Nigel stumbled through the window with Marlin and Dory and saw Nemo floating upside down in the plastic bag. The dentist quickly shooed Nigel away, but in the commotion he dropped Nemo. The bag burst open.

"I get a fishy!" squealed Darla as she reached out to grab him.

Gill flipped himself onto the tray beside Nemo.

"Tell your dad I said 'hi'," he said. Then Gill smacked his tail on a dental mirror, catapulting Nemo over Darla's waiting hands and into the spit sink. The little fish escaped down the drain!

Back in the harbour, Nigel dropped Dory and Marlin into the sea. Marlin was heartbroken. He thought that he had lost Nemo for good and swam off to be on his own.

Nemo soon met Dory. At first, she had no memory of who he was … but finally she did remember! Dory knew she had to reunite Nemo with his dad straight away!

Together, they swam after Marlin as fast as Nemo's little fins would let them.

There was a happy reunion between Marlin and Nemo. Marlin finally realized that even though Nemo was a little fish, he was capable of doing very big things! They had both learned that life was an adventure to be lived to the full.

Meanwhile, the Tank Gang were having an adventure of their own. They had finally made their escape, but now they just had to find a way to get out of the bags!